TO: James
Reading Rocks!
signature :)

Lucy and Riley love dogs of all sizes, shapes, kinds, and colors!

This book is dedicated to my wonderful children: Max, Mia, Riley, and Lucy. It's also dedicated to dog-lovers everywhere!

www.mascotbooks.com

Puppy Drama

©2016 Andra Gillum. All Rights Reserved. No part of this publication may be reproduced, stored in a retrieval system or transmitted in any form by any means electronic, mechanical, or photocopying, recording or otherwise without the permission of the author.

For more information, please contact:
Mascot Books
560 Herndon Parkway #120
Herndon, VA 20170
info@mascotbooks. com

Library of Congress Control Number: 2016908263

CPSIA Code: PRT0816A
ISBN-13: 978-1-63177-680-9

Printed in the United States

www.doggydrama.com
Contact the author: andra@doggydrama.com
Like us on Facebook: www.facebook.com/doggydrama

PUPPY DRAMA

written by Andra Gillum

illustrated by Andy Case

My name is Lucy. I'm the baby of the family. Everyone thinks I have it so good. They call me *Lucy Lucy*, but it's not so easy being me. Here's my side of the story…

This is Riley. She's my big sister, and the oldest in the family. Well, not including Mom and Dad of course. They're super old!

I think Riley is the lucky one. For years, she had Mom and Dad all to herself. She was their first born. You should see all the toys they bought her! *Can you say "spoiled rotten"?*

All of my toys are hand-me-downs from Riley. Most of them are all chewed up and covered in dog slobber! I even have to wear her old, stretched-out doggy sweaters. *I want my own stuff!*

Now that Riley is thirteen, she's gotten slower. Our long walks are cut short, and *I* have to chase all the squirrels. She's always bragging about how fast she used to be, but I'm not so sure!

Since Riley is the oldest, she always wants to be the boss. I have to throw a huge tantrum to ever get my way. She's always telling me where to go and what to do. You should see how she drags me around!

She also loves to tell me what NOT to do. "Don't eat this, don't chew that, quit rolling in mud, Mom is going to be mad…" *blah, blah, blah!*
So bossy!

She hates when I borrow her stuff! There's one special toy that I can't even touch. She guards it like it's her baby! *Who cares, Riley. I don't want your toy anyway!*

This is my big brother Max. He's twelve. Riley got to play with him when he was little and fun. Now with his video games and iPad, it's hard to even get his attention! *Hello, Max! Am I invisible?*

When he does want to play, it's always football. We have fun, but only until I flatten the ball or Max flattens me! *Easy, Max. I'm not wearing pads!*

My human big sister is named Mia. When she was a toddler, Riley got all her food from the floor. Cookies, crackers, and crumbs, oh my! Now Mia is ten, and much neater. Luckily, she does slip me a few snacks under the table!

Mia likes to pretend she's my mom. She carries me around like I'm her baby! Just because I'm small, I'm the one who gets wrapped in a blanket and hauled around the house. Put me down! *Do I look like a stuffed animal?*

Plus, Mia is totally into fashion and style. She makes me dress me up in costumes and crazy hats for her fashion shows. At least she hasn't painted my nails yet!

Everyone in the house gets to stay up later than I do. I can hear them watching TV while I'm trying to sleep!

"Oh, and did I mention how Max and Dad always try to blame me for *their* toots?"

I never get to ride in the front seat! Riley gets to sit up front while I'm stuck in the back. Mom even bought me a puppy booster seat.
How embarrassing!

Now, don't get me wrong. I do enjoy being the baby of the family! I am pretty darn cute after all, so I get lots of belly rubs. I also gets extra treats since I'm still growing.

Plus, they all watch out for me. The kids take me for nice long walks, and they even pick up my poop! *Now that's true love!*

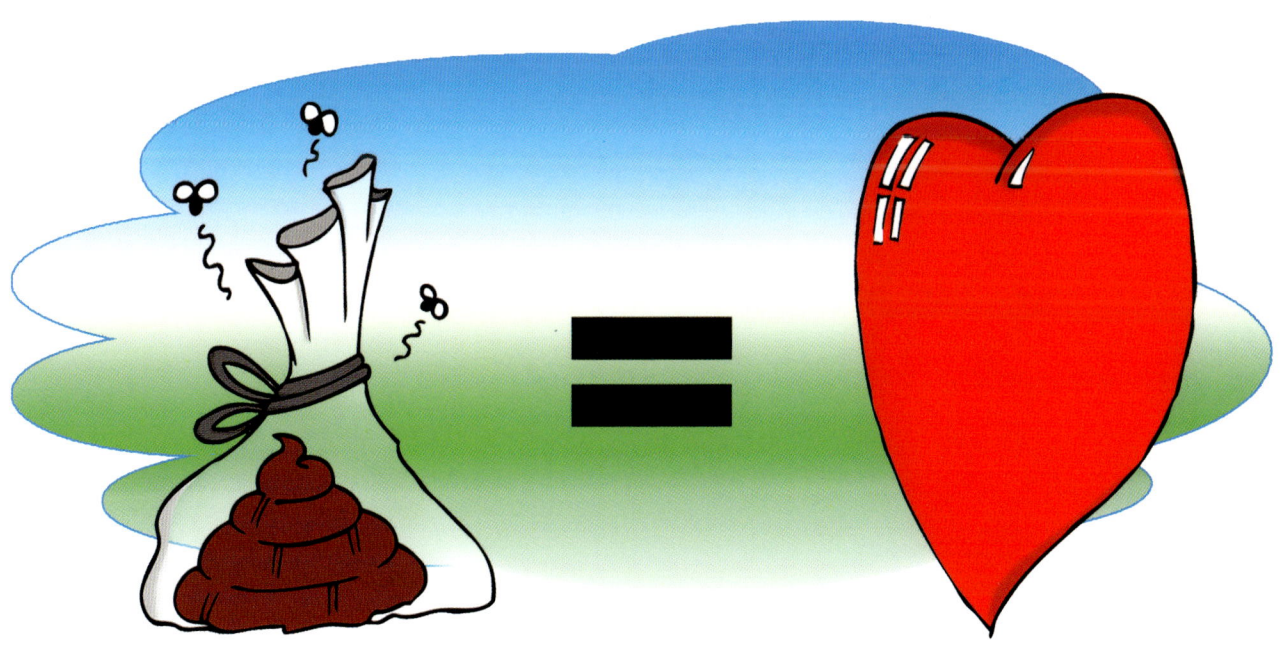

And no matter what, Riley always has my back. When I get scared, she makes me feel safe! I'm not even afraid of thunder when she's around. *Okay, maybe just a little!*

I do have a pretty great life! It's nice to have a brother and sisters who play with me and keep me safe. Just don't tell my family. I could never handle being the middle child!

Lucy enjoys reading a copy of *Doggy Drama*.

Lucy as a tiny puppy.

Riley celebrates her thirteenth birthday.

Riley as a puppy. She liked to dig!

ABOUT THE AUTHOR

Andra Gillum is a freelance writer and the author of *Doggy Drama*. She lives in Columbus, Ohio with her family.

Andra would love to hear from you!
Contact her at: andra@doggydrama.com
Or visit **www.doggydrama.com**

Have a book idea?
Contact us at:

info@mascotbooks.com | www.mascotbooks.com

www.doggydrama.com
Contact the author: andra@doggydrama.com
Like us on Facebook: www.facebook.com/doggydrama